A Double Trouble Halloween

Spread your wings and learn new things through reading.

Sandy Heitmeier Thompson

Sandy Heitmeier Thompson

Artwork by Toby Mikle

ISBN 978-1-64559-491-8 (Paperback)
ISBN 978-1-63630-823-4 (Hardcover)
ISBN 978-1-64559-492-5 (Digital)

Covenant Books, Inc.
11661 Hwy 707
Murrells Inlet, SC 29576
www.covenantbooks.com

I felt lucky and very
blessed because
my students to me
were the best.

Each child was special
and one of a kind.
The goodness in them
was easy to find.

I thank them from the
bottom of my heart. They
made my teaching career
meaningful from the start.

Now, I get to see many
of them all grown. I am
so proud of them as if
they were my own.

It was a crisp, cool Sunday in autumn. The weather had been getting cooler. Days were growing shorter, and nights longer. Leaves were changing colors and falling off trees.

Ann asked her two sons, Brett and Blake, if they would help rake the leaves outside the house. The boys agreed. First, the boys decided to rake the leaves into a few piles. That way it would be easier to put the leaves in bags and set them on the curb to be picked up.

After a couple of hours, Ann called out, "Boys, take a break. Lunch is ready."

The boys ran inside, washed their hands, and sat down at the kitchen table. Then their mom served them cheese pizza, fruit, and juice.

When the boys were finished eating, they thanked their mom. They then went back outside to complete their chore.

"Look!" exclaimed Blake as he walked out the front door. "The leaves aren't in piles anymore. They're all scattered again!"

"That's strange. There's no wind. I wonder what happened," Brett replied.

Soon the boys' friend Gavin approached them.

"Hey, guys," he said. "What's up? Why do you look confused?"

The boys told Gavin about the mystery of the scattered leaves.

"Well," said Gavin, "in a couple days it will be Halloween night, and strange things tend to happen."

"I'm not sure if I believe all that spooky nonsense," stated Brett.

"Well, I do!" exclaimed Blake. Blake was a couple of years younger than Brett, so he was understandably more easily frightened.

The three boys did not notice two black ravens chuckling to themselves as they sat atop a nearby roof. Ren and his cousin Razz loved to be mischievous and cause chaos.

"We can have lots of fun with these humans," Ren snickered.

"We sure can!" replied Razz.

The next day at school, Blake's teacher, Ms. Helm, decided to teach her class about the history of Halloween.

"On November first," she explained, "many churches in our country celebrate All Saints' Day. Christians consider saints to be holy people who devoted their lives to helping others. Some have suffered and died for their beliefs. That day is sometimes called All Hallows Day because hallow means holy. Halloween, October thirty-first, is the eve of All Hallows' Day."

"Why do children dress in costumes, especially as monsters?" asked Maya. Maya was a very bright student in Blake's class. She was also one of Blake's best friends.

Ms. Helm explained, "Long ago, people believed that on Halloween night, ghosts could contact the physical world. People thought that the spirits' magic was the most powerful on Halloween night. Perhaps dressing up as monstrous creatures, such as mummies, witches, or vampires, was a way to scare away the evil spirits and prevent people from being harmed."

Ms. Helm could see that her students were fascinated, so she continued her lecture. "Halloween is very popular in Ireland, where it is said to have originated. People would light bonfires to ward off the demons. At first, instead of pumpkins, people would carve turnips and place candles inside them."

Time flew by, and soon the dismissal bell rang.

"That lesson was so intriguing," Maya told Blake as they left the classroom. "I'm going to find out more about Halloween."

"I'm going with my brother and Gavin to a pumpkin patch to pick out some pumpkins so we can carve them into jack-o-lanterns. Would you like to join us?" asked Blake.

"Yes!" answered Maya. "I'm sure my mom will give me permission to go. I'll meet you at your house in an hour."

Later, all four kids walked to the nearby pumpkin patch. There were all different sizes of pumpkins there, so each kid could pick the perfect pumpkin to carve.

Meanwhile, the ravens Ren and Razz were in a tree close by.

"I think it's time for another Halloween prank," Razz giggled.

The playful ravens found a large pumpkin and used their beaks to hollow it out. When the kids were not looking, Razz placed the entire pumpkin over Ren, pushed it close to the kids, then perched herself on a branch hidden from view.

Suddenly, the kids heard a spooky, ghostly voice say, *"Boo! I see you!"* Just then a pumpkin mysteriously started moving toward them.

Blake yelled, "I'm getting out of here!"

Frightened, the four kids began running home as fast as they could.

After traveling a short distance, Brett shouted, "Hold up, gang! Something doesn't seem right!"

Gavin agreed. "I was thinking the same thing," he said. "Let's sneak back and investigate the situation."

Maya and Blake did not like this idea, but they reluctantly followed the two older boys.

When the kids got back to the pumpkin patch, they saw the two ravens rolling on the ground, laughing and chatting about their pranks. The birds were cackling so hard they didn't even notice the children approach.

Brett said, "Let's go to my house and make a plan to teach those two rascals a lesson."

"Yeah!" Gavin responded. "Tomorrow is Halloween, so you know those two mischief makers will try to scare us again."

In Brett and Blake's yard, the kids sat at a picnic table and discussed some ideas. Maya had the best plan. She suggested they unwrap several pieces of Halloween candy, put hot pepper sauce on each piece, rewrap the candy, and put them in a special trick-or-treat bag.

Blake laughed and said, "Then when the ravens try to scare us, I can drop the bag before running away. I'm sure those troublemakers won't be able to resist a bundle of sweets to eat."

Brett and Gavin praised the two younger kids for coming up with such a great plan. The schemers got straight to work preparing their special candy bag.

Soon it was Halloween night. Everyone met at Gavin's house. The four companions decided to dress in traditional Halloween costumes. Gavin was a vampire, Maya was a witch, Blake was a ghost, and Brett was a mummy.

Ms. Tara, Gavin's mom, giggled as she got the kids together for a picture.

"Now remember, always check out your surroundings, stay together, and look out for one another. Call me right away if you need me," lectured Ms. Tara.

The four spooky creatures agreed and then went out to enjoy the fun.

While the kids were trick-or-treating, the ravens were planning their next hoax. For it they would need a pair of men's shoes. Sure enough they found just what they were looking for on someone's front porch. The bandits swooped down, grabbed the shoes in their beaks, and headed to find their victims.

Later, the children finished trick-or-treating and began heading back to their homes. Suddenly, they heard loud footsteps behind them. The birds were using the stolen shoes to make stomping sounds. Then a screechy voice said, "Hocus pocus, zimminey zan, run away from this goblin as fast as you can!"

The kids pretended to be scared. They screamed and started running. Just as planned, Blake dropped the special candy bag on the ground. Then he and the other kids hid in some nearby bushes.

The ravens could not stop laughing.
Razz exclaimed, "Those kids are dummies!"
Chuckling, Ren added, "Yep, they sure are a bunch of morons."

26

Razz spotted the bag and said, "Well, look what we have here. It's a bag of goodies for all our hard work."

"Yummy! There's nothing like a delicious reward for a job well done," Ren said with a smirk on his face.

Both ravens removed the candy wrappers and began devouring the treats.

Just then Razz started screaming. "Help! Help!" she shouted. "My tongue is on fire!"

Ren yelled, "I can't take the scorching in my mouth. Call the fire department!"

The kids came out from their hiding places. Now it was their turn to enjoy a victory.

They did not want the birds to suffer too much, so Brett and Gavin handed Razz and Ren each a pint of milk. They knew that drinking milk provided relief after eating something spicy.

Maya looked straight at the birds. Grinning slyly, she teased, "Birds of a feather should not plot together!"

Blake then ended the night by calling out, 'Hocus, pocus, zimminey zan, drink that milk as fast as you can!"

About the Author

Some of Sandy's favorite times as an educator were celebrating special days and holidays with her young students. They were always excited and cheerful. Their feelings were contagious. Mrs. Thompson always felt excited with them. She made sure they sang songs, played games, made crafts, etc. to enhance the season and the excitement of waiting for that special day.

Halloween was one of the first fun days to celebrate. The kids loved all the activities leading up to that "spooky day." Mrs. Thompson made sure the classroom was accessorized with a Halloween theme. The students decorated mini pumpkins for a contest. For art, they cut and colored a witch on a broom, glued together a skeleton made out of paper bones, and drew a haunted house while listening to scary sounds of Halloween. The children really loved making a witch's brew out of fruit punch and dried ice for a science experiment.

The parents, friends, and relatives put together a small trick or treat festival for the whole school. The children got to wear costumes and disguise themselves for the day. The teachers enjoyed watching the older students help out the younger students.

No one ever thought of Halloween as a day to worship a demon, devil, or any evil creature. That thought never entered anyone's mind. Most kids think Halloween is a day to dress up, eat candy, and have fun with family and friends.

It is nice to see the world through children's eyes. Kids are usually sweet, innocent, and do not have hatred in their hearts. They are such a delight to be around.

CPSIA information can be obtained
at www.ICGtesting.com
Printed in the USA
BVHW020913050321
601078BV00005B/20

9 781636 308234